THIS BOOK BELONGS TO

....

....

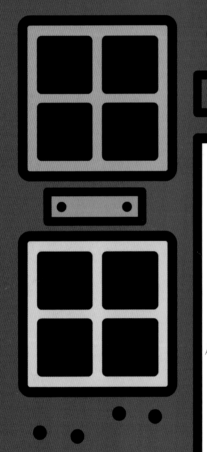

HEY
DUGGEE

LADYBIRD BOOKS

UK | USA | Canada | Ireland | Australia | India | New Zealand | South Africa
Ladybird Books is part of the Penguin Random House group of companies
whose addresses can be found at global.penguinrandomhouse.com.
www.penguin.co.uk   www.puffin.co.uk   www.ladybird.co.uk

 Penguin
Random House
UK

First published 2023
001
Text and illustrations copyright © Studio AKA Limited, 2023
Adapted by Rebecca Gerlings, based on "Happy's First Day Badge", "Tag's First Day Badge",
"Betty's First Day Badge", "Roly's First Day Badge" and "Norrie's First Day Badge"
written by James Walsh
Printed in China
The authorized representative in the EEA is Penguin Random House Ireland,
Morrison Chambers, 32 Nassau Street, Dublin D02 YH68
A CIP catalogue record for this book is available from the British Library
ISBN: 978-1-405-95428-0
All correspondence to:
Ladybird Books, Penguin Random House Children's
One Embassy Gardens, 8 Viaduct Gardens, London SW11 7BW

FIRST DAY
AT SQUIRREL CLUB

NORRIE   ROLY   DUGGEE   HAPPY   TAG   BETTY

Today at the clubhouse, the Squirrels are playing hot grass. They have to jump all the way across the garden to the final rock without touching the ground.

After hot grass, the Squirrels play bouncing mushrooms . . .

elephant slide . . .

find the potato . . .

and mice in a row!

"Ah-woof!" says Duggee proudly.
The clubhouse hasn't always been so busy. On Norrie's first day, she was the only Squirrel!
"First day?" asks Betty. "Haven't we *always* come to Squirrel Club?"

Duggee shakes his head. He remembers each Squirrel's first day at the clubhouse. He has his **First Day Badge!**
Back then, the Squirrels were a *lot* younger . . .

On Norrie's first day, she arrived with her parents and all seventy-two of her little brothers and sisters.

It was the first time Norrie had ever met Duggee, and she had the clubhouse all to herself. It was lots of fun!

But there are only so many things you can do by yourself. Norrie missed having someone to play with.

Luckily, Duggee had an idea! He took Norrie to meet all the animals who live around the clubhouse.

There was Frog, who liked to croak ...

RIBBIT!

and the chickens, who laid eggs. Lots of eggs.

BACAW!

Cow gave the Squirrel Club milk – from her udder!

WIBBLE-WOBBLE!

The sheep had lovely soft, woolly coats.

BAA!

Worm knew a lot about the weather.

SPLISH! SPLASH!

Goldfish had a very bubbly personality.

BLUB! BLUB!

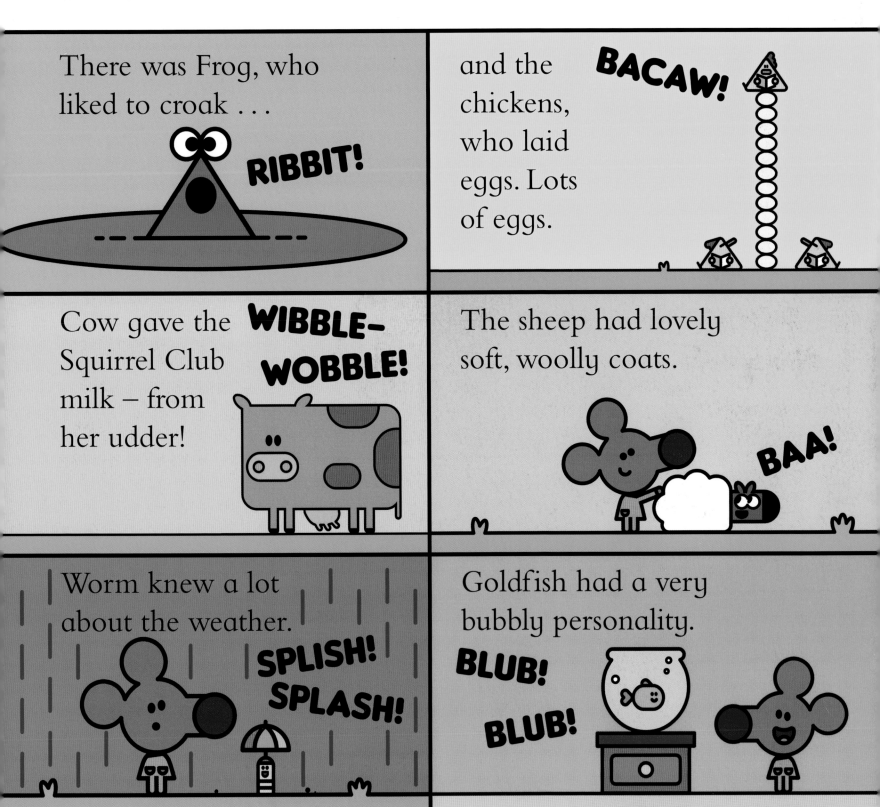

Finally, there was Enid the kitten. At first, she was a bit shy . . .

but she and Norrie soon became best friends.

AWW! HOW SWEET!

And it wasn't long before Norrie had another friend to play with ... Roly! On Roly's first day at Squirrel Club, he was *quite* different from how he is today.

WAS I?

"Ah-woof!" Duggee remembers ...

When Roly arrived at Squirrel Club, he was very quiet.
He hardly spoke a word!

Roly didn't want to let go of his dad.

DAAAAAAD!

Duggee thought perhaps a friend might help . . .

HI!

"But where were *we*?" asks Tag.

Duggee explains that Tag, Happy and Betty are younger than Norrie and Roly. They hadn't started at Squirrel Club yet!

"Did Roly and I play together?" asks Norrie.

"Woof woof," replies Duggee.
Not at first . . .

But then Duggee had another idea!
He got Norrie and Roly to do things together . . .

and that helped
Roly settle in!
Almost.

DAAADDYYY!

That's when Duggee noticed that Roly had a particularly nice voice. He wanted to hear more.
"What else can you say?" asked Roly's dad.

Soon, Roly was having so much fun being himself that he hardly noticed his dad leaving at all.

And he's carried on being himself ever since.

Then, one day, Happy joined Squirrel Club too. Together, Roly and Norrie showed Happy how to have fun on *his* first day. They played with toys . . .

made music . . .

and helped Duggee.

"I remember!" says Norrie.
"You were so . . ."
"HAPPY!" shouts Roly.

AH-WOOF!

That same afternoon, all three
Squirrels went for a walk and
splashed in some puddles.

UH-OH!

Duggee could see that Happy wasn't happy about splashing
in the puddles. He was scared of them!

It wasn't just puddles that made Happy nervous . . .
anything watery did.

Poor Happy!
"But you like water now," says Betty.
"Ah-woof woof!" Duggee agrees.
That's because his new friends
helped him to overcome his fear.

Little by little, Roly and Norrie showed Happy there was nothing to worry about.

And he started to see how *amazing* water is!

You can clean things with it ...

play with it ...

drink it ...

and some animals live in it.

Ever since then, Happy has *loved* water!

SPLASH!

SPLASH!

Which is a good thing, because when Tag joined Squirrel Club there was a watery near miss that could have been a disaster!

"Ah-woof!" says Duggee. He remembers it well.

You see, Tag wasn't always as good at listening as he is now. On his first day at Squirrel Club, he got stuck in straight away.

He clearly didn't lack confidence. Everyone was impressed.

Actually, Tag had so much, er, *enthusiasm* that Duggee had to decide whether or not he could stay at Squirrel Club.

"Oh no!" cries Norrie.
"Tag had to leave?" asks Betty.
"But he's our friend," says Happy.
"I'm SAD," says Roly.
Not to worry, Squirrels. Duggee had an idea!

Duggee told Tag that when he was little he'd had trouble listening too.

AH-WOOF WOOF, WOOF . . .

At first, it was hard to get Tag's attention. But Duggee knew his story would help.

WOOF WOOF, WOOF . . .

WOOF WOOF, WOOF WOOF!

And eventually it did! Tag learned that listening can keep you safe, lead to good things and make sure you don't miss out!

Listening can also make you feel included, which is what Betty found out on her first day at Squirrel Club.
When Betty arrived, she preferred to play on her own.

WHY DIDN'T SHE WANT TO PLAY WITH US?

"Woof woof," replies Duggee. Betty just did things her own way.

Betty was used to playing alone.

What do you think happened next, Squirrels?

"Ah-woof!" says Duggee.
Yes, Duggee taught the Squirrels the Squirrel Club song,
so they would feel like a team!

THERE'S A SPECIAL PLACE,
WHERE WE LOVE TO BE.
IT'S WHERE WE ALL HAVE FUN . . .
IT'S SQUIRREL CLUB!
WHERE WE DO LOTS OF THINGS
AT SQUIRREL CLUB!
WE PLAY, DANCE AND SING
AT SQUIRREL CLUB!
LET'S ALL JOIN IN
AT SQUIRREL CLUB!

The song had a special verse for each Squirrel –
including the newest Squirrel, Betty!

**THERE'S AN OCTOPUS
WITH A BRILLIANT BRAIN,
WHO'S SUNNY AND FUNNY
AND SHE'S OUR NEW FRIEND!**

Duggee sighs happily.

The Squirrel Club song brought everyone together, and they spent the rest of the day having *lots* of fun.

"We love Squirrel Club!" shout the Squirrels.

"And I love playing with my friends!" says Betty.

"Me too!" says Roly.

Aww, that was a lot of fun remembering all those first days, wasn't it, Duggee? And, Squirrels, you all earned your **First Day Badges!**

Now there's just time for one last thing
before the Squirrels go home . . .

"DUGGEE HUG!"